Sea Creatures from the Sky

Written and Illustrated by
Ricardo Cortés

*T*his is a tale of
no one believing
something that is
entirely true…

…has that ever happened to you?

Not a fib, not a fable, nor a stretch of reality.

This really, really, really, really happened to me.

There is a strange beast that lives in the air.

That's the story I'm here to share.

It came from above the sea.

Above me.

Don't be absurd.

It was no bird.

There is something else,
and that's no lie.

It stole me from the ocean,
and took me to the sky.

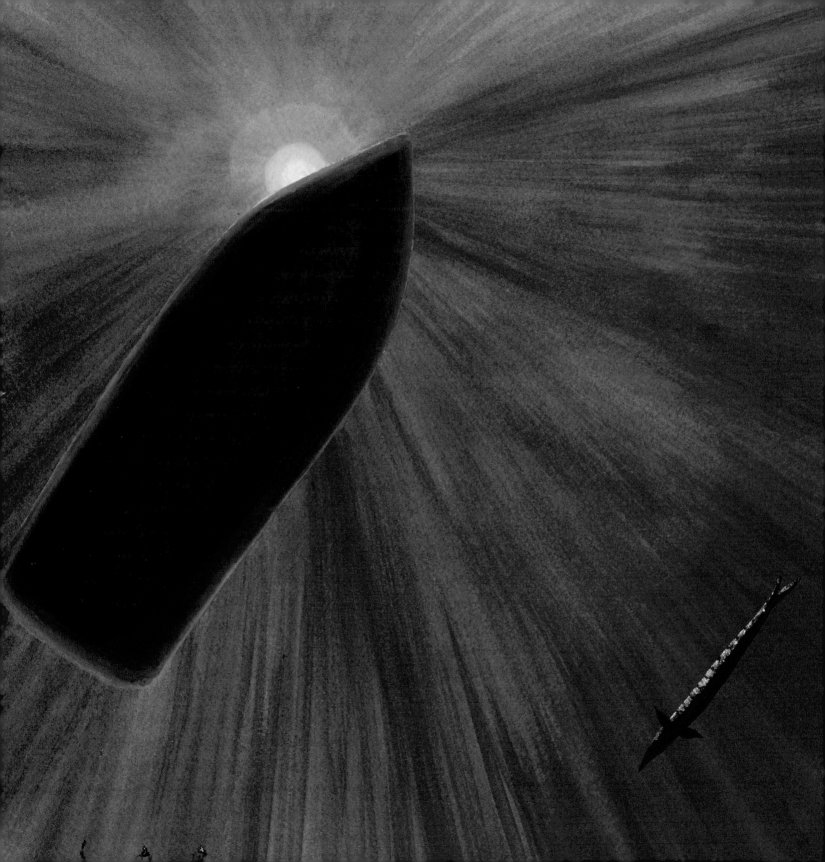

The first time I saw it, it rumbled by
without saying *hello* or even *hi*.

Maybe it was shy.

The second time it stopped and I thought,
Now we shall meet.

But then I saw a fresh little fish to eat.

One bite,
that's all it took.

For this little fish had a hook.

I should warn you about the next page.

Because if you look, you might scream.

I saw the two scariest creatures I've ever seen.

They measured.

They probed.

They spoke in a strange code.

Do you believe me so far?
Because you would be alone.

I knew no one would buy this story
when I got home.

Everyone I told, from the whale
to anchovies, scoffed at the tale
as a "complete impossibility."

In ships they steered?

Faces with beards?

Heads with two ears?

It was all just too weird.

So I sulked, and swam, and I did not speak.

I felt like my tale made me a freak.

And then after some time, maybe two weeks,
I came to accept that life is unique.

I know what I saw with my very own eye.

Creatures in the sky.

The End

RICARDO CORTÉS has written and illustrated books about tomatoes, grass, the history of coffee, and Coca-Cola. He is the illustrator of a #1 *New York Times* best-selling classic for parents about putting their children to bed, as well as the G-rated follow-up, *Seriously, Just Go to Sleep*. He lives in Brooklyn, New York, and on **Rmcortes.com**.

Published by Akashic Books
©2018 Ricardo Cortés
ISBN: 978-1-61775-616-0
Library of Congress Control Number: 2017956180

First printing
Printed in Malaysia

Black Sheep/Akashic Books
Brooklyn, New York, USA
Ballydehob, Co. Cork, Ireland
Twitter: @AkashicBooks
Facebook: AkashicBooks
E-mail: info@akashicbooks.com
Website: www.akashicbooks.com